"I tell you the truth, anyone who doesn't receive the Kingdom of God like a child will never enter it." Mark 10:15

When kids ask about Jesus, we often tell them things like "Jesus died on the cross for your sins" or "Jesus took our sins away." These can be confusing truths for children. As well, we often skirt the uglier truths about what happened to Jesus as he walked the Earth. We do so for fear that these truths are too much for a child. Yet, we've already let the cat out of the bag when we tell kids Bible stories that are unavoidably gritty, graphic and quite a bit more than rated G.

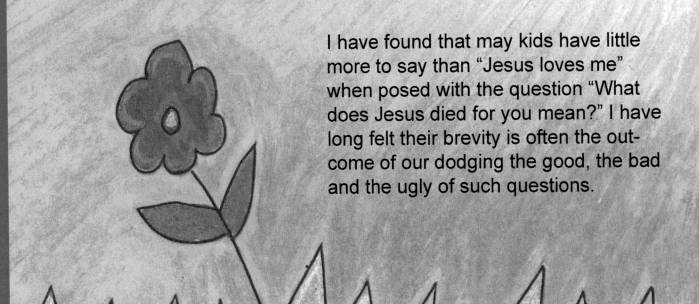

I have found that may kids have little more to say than "Jesus loves me" when posed with the question "What does Jesus died for you mean?" I have long felt their brevity is often the out-come of our dodging the good, the bad and the ugly of such questions.

We mean well in our efforts to protect a child's innocence, but I have learned that there is fallout for this. Children are getting baptized, receiving communion and are participating in other sacraments with much prepared hearts but less ready minds. It doesn't have to be this way. Children can have a deeper understanding of the mysteries presented to them through God's word and His church. We don't have to be afraid to give the whole story, and we don't have to assume that kids can't understand the unabridged version. Children are asking the really hard questions, and they are ready to welcome these truths of God's kingdom like a child. It is my prayer that **Jesus for Kids** will help children dig a little deeper, straighten confusions, and address questions (as well as fears) about who Jesus is. By the grace of God, I pray they will receive revelation, peace and truth.

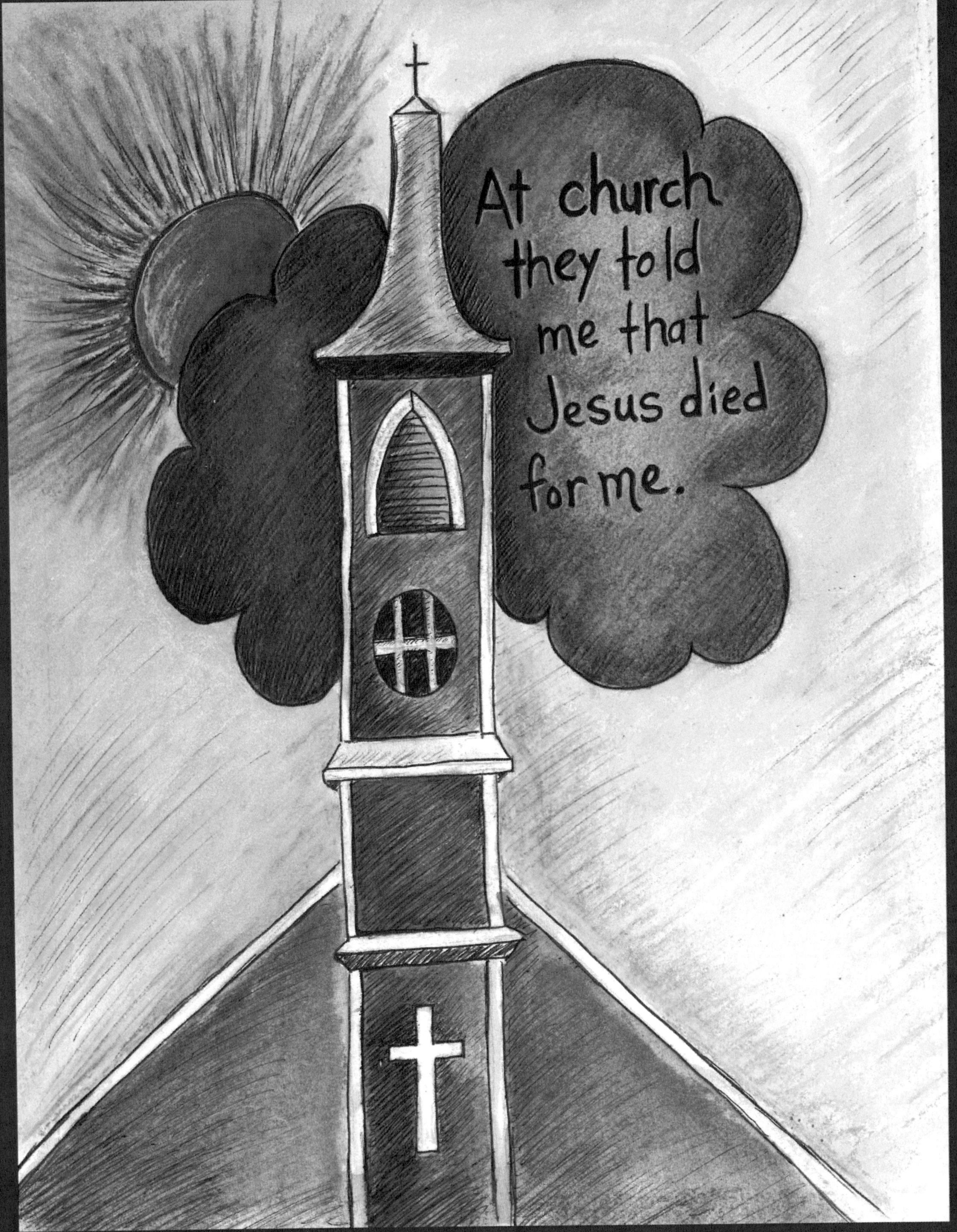
At church they told me that Jesus died for me.

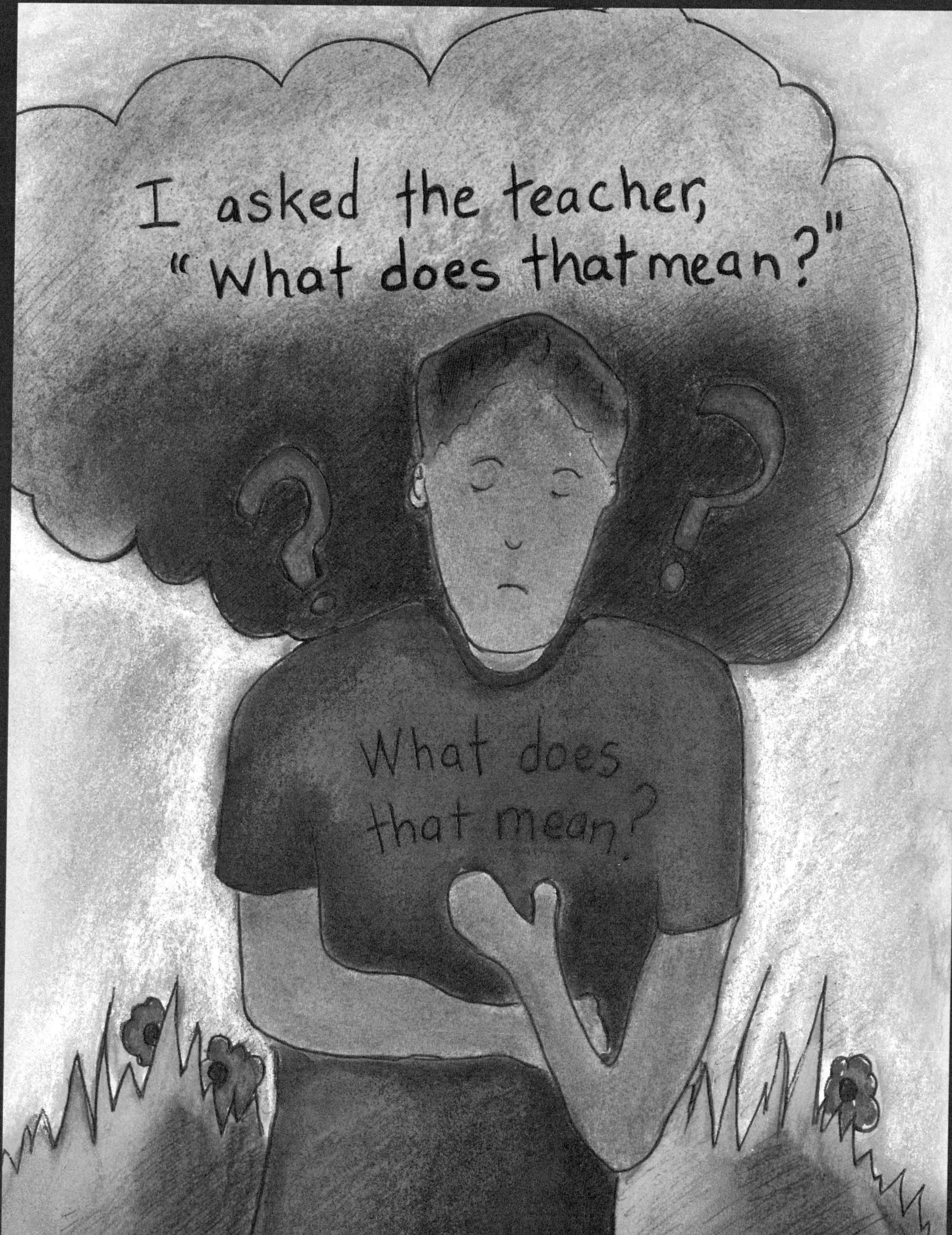

Jesus died to take your sins away.
Her answer left me with even more questions.
I still don't get it.
confused

I decided to ask my mom for help.
She always knows how to keep things SIMPLE.
CONFUSED

Mom could see that I was really scratching my head.
What does "Jesus died for me" mean?
Confused
Mom
Mom

My older sister listened too. I guess.
I'm curious to hear what Mom has to say.
she was curious??????
Curious

"He was a special man : both human and God at the same time. The man's name was Jesus."

Special

..."He became a man – a human – so we'd know that He totally understood what it's like to be a person: what it's
like to love, to feel pain and to feel joy – just like us...."
Like you and me!
Just like us!

"Jesus putting Himself in a human's body was a huge chance to take."
"Becoming human meant that Jesus would have to know all the hard stuff about being a person."
Mom

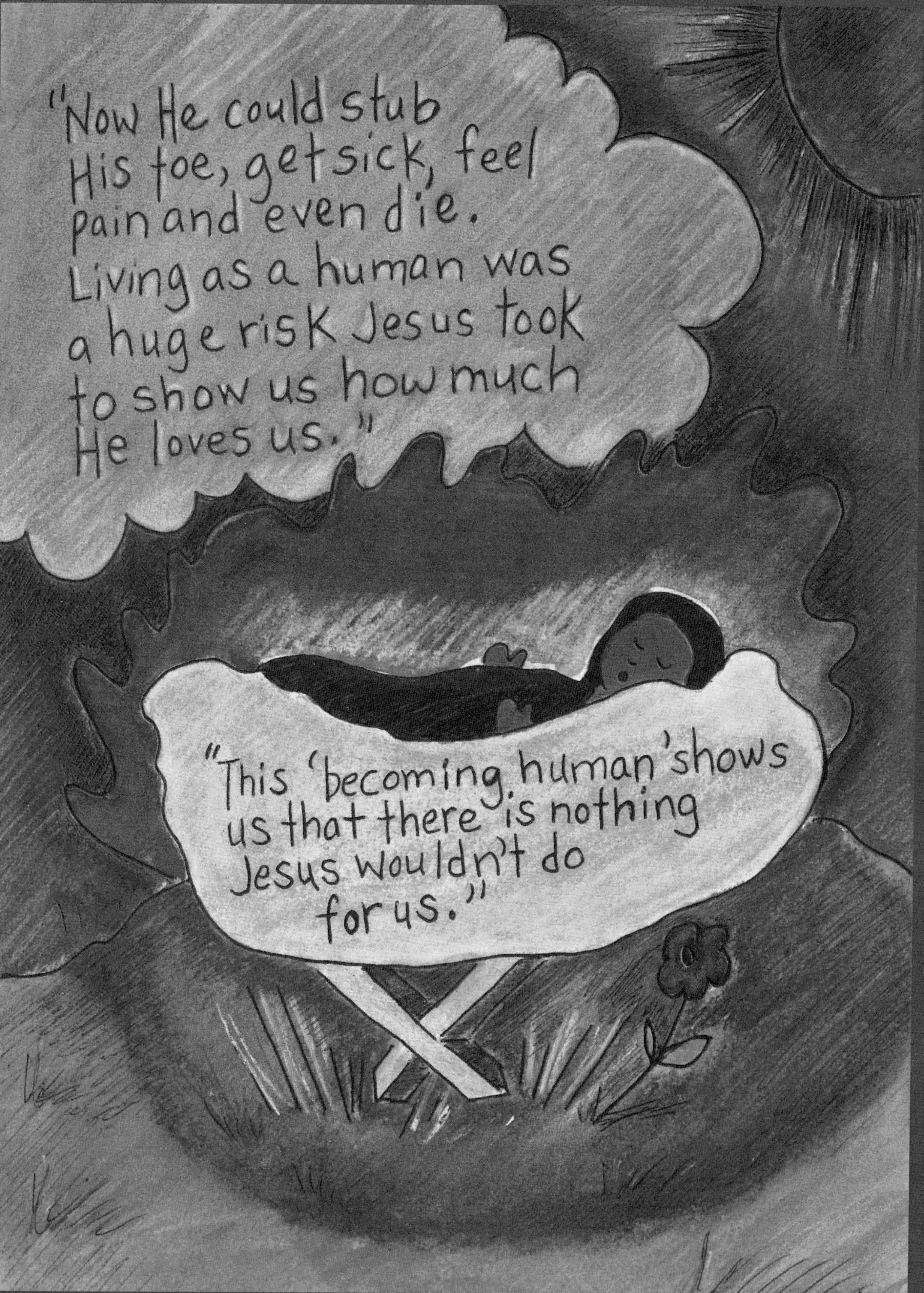
"Now He could stub His toe, get sick, feel pain and even die. Living as a human was a huge risk Jesus took to show us how much He loves us."
"This 'becoming human' shows us that there is nothing Jesus wouldn't do for us."

Mom told us more.
"Jesus grew up and became a man."
"He spoke the truth and some people really didn't like it."
Mom
Mom
Confused ? ?
Curious ? ?

"He spoke God's truth and many people didn't want to listen."
Give all your things to the poor and come follow Me.
Shut up! Don't say that or else!

The people with power wanted all the power for themselves. Jesus was messing with their plans..."
I am the ONLY King!

Mom explained how Jesus forgives.
"The weak, the poor and the hungry loved Jesus and He loved them too. He loved children. He healed the sick. And, best of all, He forgave people's sins."
"No matter what you did or how big your sins, Jesus forgave."
Your sins are forgiven.
"He forgave when people asked and believed."

Mom used the Bible to explain how Jesus died for us...
Jesus dying on the cross shows us that there's nothing Jesus wouldn't do for us or forgive us for. NOTHING!
Mom
Mom
"The Bible tells the story of how humans killed Jesus in a really awful way. It also tells us how Jesus invited us to be with Him anyway."

OK!
NO!
"The Bible tells
the story of how Jesus
died on a terrible cross, in a
terrible way, between 2 terrible
men. One of the men said "OK"
to knowing Jesus and he got to be
with Jesus that very day. The
other man said "No thanks" to
Knowing Jesus and to Heaven.
That was that man's own choice.
Jesus sadly accepted it."

"Jesus died for you: for all of us. He did it to show you and me that killing Him isn't enough to make Him give up on us. The human race killed God (in a human's body) and God did not give up on us! Jesus died so that we would understand that His love for us can be this incredibly deep."

"God's love is a mystery that's so huge that He will even forgive the most awful things..."
I really don't know how God can forgive like that.
Mom
Mom
"But..."

"You must..."
"Want a relationship with God."
"Accept Jesus into your life and trust that He is God's son."
"Ask for forgiveness for the things you did wrong on purpose; that's sin."
"Love others and forgive them as God has done for you."

"Never forget that...
God's love is NEVER earned.
"You can't do more good things..."
"You can't make more right choices..."
"and"
"You can't work harder to get more of God's love."
"You are simply His child and He will always love you!"

Mom, this is really too good to be true.
Curious!
And very hard to understand.
Confused
It is truly a mystery.
Mom
Mom
"We aren't meant to fully understand, but it is true nonetheless!"

This is the part where FAITH comes in.
"Faith is all about trust. You can trust a Father who loves you with such unbelieveable love. You can trust his forgiveness. You can trust all the ways His son's death proves how immensely He loves You. Jesus died so your faith and trust in God could be sure. It's all the proof you need. There is no greater love."
Mom
Mom

"Your faith and trust is the most beautiful gift you can offer God."
Jesus, help me have faith in you.
Faith
Help me trust your love.
Trust
Mom
"And, help us all understand the gift you gave us when you died for us."
Mom

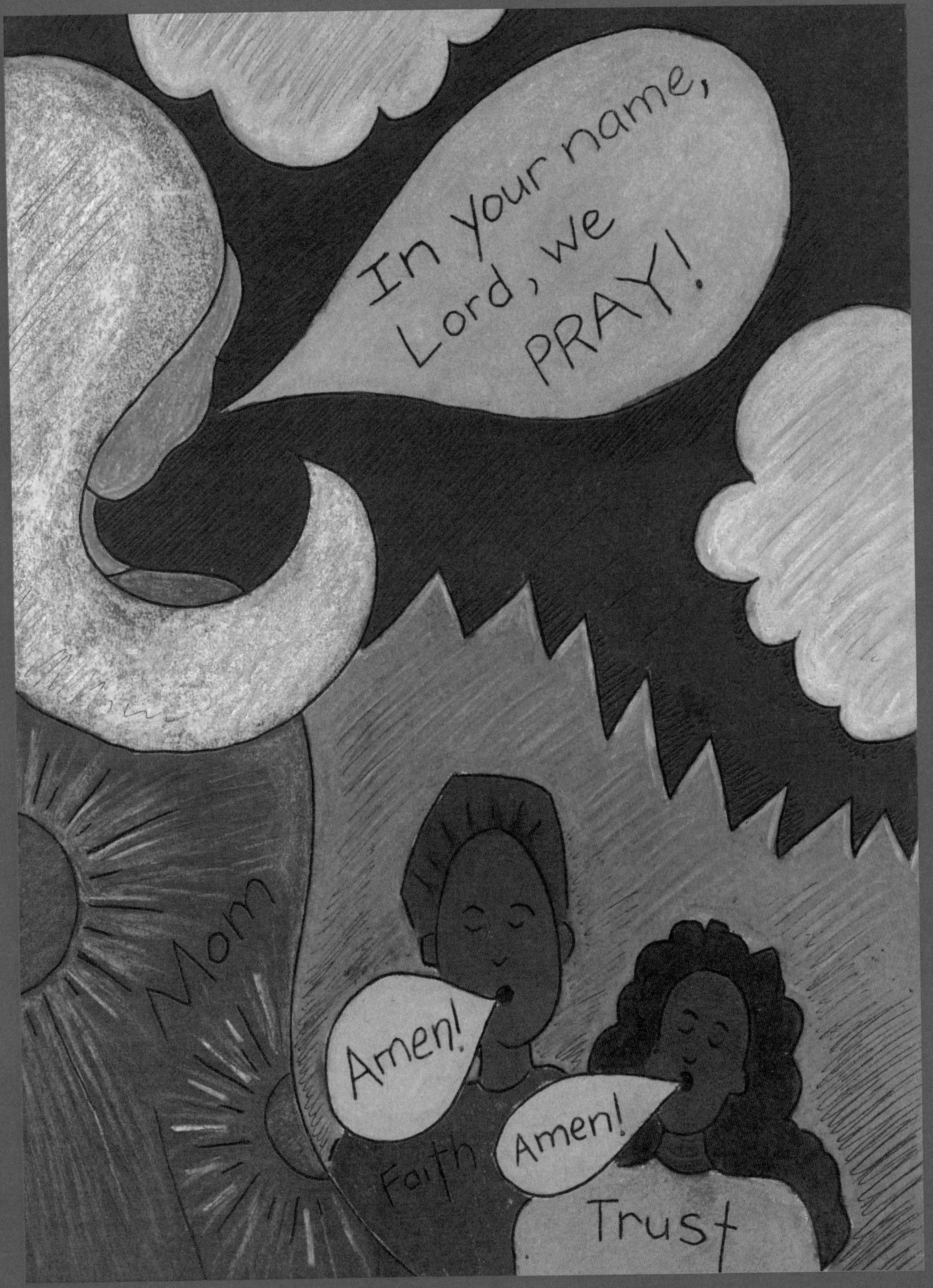
In your name, Lord, we PRAY!
Mom
Amen!
Amen!
Faith
Trust

This book is dedicated to all the kids who keep on asking the really hard questions.

Printed by CreateSpace, an Amazon.com Company
Available from Amazon.Com and Other Bookstores
Bulk orders can be purchased through www.JourneyOnCanvas.com
ISBN-13: 978-1543044126
ISBN-10: 1543044123

For many years, Alisa has helped teach kids about Jesus: on a Sunday morning, at a VBS, or at a church event. While teaching a simple Bible lesson or just spending time with kids at these events, conversations about God would bring children to ask some pretty hard questions. Alisa wrote and illustrated *Jesus for Kids* to give simple and tangible answers to these types of questions without compromising their deeper truths. She hopes this book will give young seekers some of the answers they have asked for.

Alisa also authored and illustrated *Guardian Angels: A Book about Angels for Children*. This brightly illustrated children's book shows young people the ways God is with them during the ordinary, everyday moments of their lives. Alisa hopes this book will help kids face a myriad of common fears and experience joy.

You can learn more about Alisa on her website at www.JourneyOnCanvas.com. All of Alisa's books can be purchased on Amazon.com.

Made in the USA
Columbia, SC
05 May 2023

16128979R00022